THIS BOOK BELONGS TO

_____

Welcome to Middle School

Welcome to Middle School

A 6th Grade Super Hero Middle School Chapter Book

Copyright 2020

Emery Trax

ISBN: 9781537434384

Independently Published

1

Next to forgetting your school locker combination, feeling dazed and confused is the worst thing ever.

I know.

Because you see, I live in the state of confusion. I blame my mom for always waking me up too early in the morning. Like on the first day of school...

"Jason James Coldwater, wake up, now," my mom shouted from downstairs.

"I hear you," I shouted back. "The whole neighborhood can hear you."

And while I have been known to stretch a story for dramatic effect, I wasn't exaggerating on that one.

Last summer a neighbor who lives across the street told me he stopped using an alarm clock.

"No need," he said and pointed to my mom who was busy helping my little sister Jessie set up a lemonade stand. "I hear her yelling at you every morning, six a.m. sharp."

I checked the clock on my nightstand and groaned. Sure enough, it was six in the morning.

"Take Charger on his walk before breakfast," mom said and opened the back door.

I felt the loop of the leash slip over my hand and half a second later did a face plant on the back porch when Charger bolted for the newspaper boy.

"Control your dog," the newspaper boy shouted and pulled a canister of pepper spray from his pocket.

But it was too late.

Charger jerked the leash looped around my wrist and lunged.

"Back," the newspaper boy screeched and pressed the juice button on his pepper spray.

"Yeow," I screamed and rubbed my eyes. "My eyes are on fire."

"That's what you get," the newspaper boy snarled and zipped down the sidewalk on his bicycle.

Unfazed by the pepper spray attack, Charger dragged me to the street, paused long enough to allow a delivery truck to get closer, and then darted into traffic.

I guess you could say being blinded by pepper spray was a good thing, because truthfully, nobody, especially me, needed to see the chaos Charger created as he raced across the four lanes of Honey Buckle Road.

I remember hearing car horns, the screech of brakes, the sounds of mean voices screaming something about staying out of the road, and the crunching sound of bumpers banging together, followed by the distant sound of a siren, and my mom yelling for me to come get my breakfast.

"I nearly got run over out there," I mumbled as I shoved my head under the kitchen water faucet. "Oh, thank you, sweet water."

"How you manage to get into trouble at six in the morning is beyond me," my mom said and stared out the kitchen window. "Sure seems like a lot of confusion out on Honey Buckle this morning. I do wish people would watch where they go. Somebody's going to get run over one day."

"Yeah, like today," I said and dried my stinging eyes. I was having trouble focusing. "This is great. The first day of 6th grade, and I'll be seeing double until at least lunch period. I just love pepper spray for breakfast."

"That's nice, dear," my mom said and splashed milk into a bowl of corn flakes for my little sister, Jessie.

"Try not to get sent to the principal's office your first day," Jessie said and stuck her tongue out at me.

"Jessie, leave your brother alone and eat your corn flakes."

"Yuck! I hate corn flakes," Jessie said and slipped the bowl to Charger, who practically lived under her chair. "Corn flakes give me morning breath, all day long."

Welcome to middle school, I thought and pored myself a bowl of morning breath cereal.

2

"Welcome to Weedhaven. 6th graders step to the right. Keep moving, please," a bored man in a red and yellow polka dotted bow tie said. "Welcome to Weedhaven. Keep moving. Nothing to see here, folks..."

"Can you believe they pay that guy?" my best friend, Emery Trax, said. "I mean, why not just put up a little sign that says, middle school victims...step to the right for your initiation?"

"He's like one of those door greeters at a warehouse shopping club," I said and surveyed the chaos in the main hall of Weedhaven Middle School.

"Yeah, but no free cookie samples," Emery replied. "Oh no, don't look now."

Of course, whenever anybody says "don't look," what they really mean is, LOOK. So naturally, I looked.

"Jake Pensor," I said.

Jake Pensor was a notorious bully, who according to rumor control failed the 5th grade three times before finally making it into middle school. The guy was big enough to play right tackle for the NFL, and ugly enough to be mistaken as an alien.

"Poor aliens," Emery said.

Weird. Sometimes I wondered if Emery could read my mind or something. "You mean poor us," I said. "He's coming this way."

"Let's start this new school year on the right foot," Jake said and dropped his book bag on Emery's foot. "Coldwater, where's my peanut butter sandwich?"

"Did you order a peanut butter sandwich?" I asked. Jake and I had an understanding. Thanks to my reading skills, and Jake's math skills, we managed to help each other squeak through summer school and pass the 5th grade. We were almost pals—in a tortured bully versus victim sort of way.

"Don't get wise?" Jake scowled and cast a suspicious stare at Emery. "You didn't tell him about my reading problem, did you?"

"Who me?" I said. "That's our little secret. Although, I think maybe you just let the cat out of the bag."

"What cat?" Jake said and looked up and down the hall. "I did not put Mrs. Bumpersnickel's claw happy, walking hairball of a cat in the school gymnasium."

"Relax," I said. "It's just a figure of speech. It means you let the secret out."

"Oh, yeah," Jake said and punched my shoulder. "Next time speak normal like, and bring me a peanut butter sandwich. You wouldn't want me to miss breakfast—would you?"

3

"Good morning, 6th graders," the man in the red and yellow polka dotted bow tie said to about a hundred screaming 6th graders assembled in the school gymnasium. "My name is Principal Thaddeus P. Thornton."

"Did he say his name is Principal?" Emery whispered. "What kind of mom names their kid principal?"

"It means he's the principal," I said. People are always confusing their job titles with their first names."

"Oh," Emery said. "But, what happened to Principal Hoehum's wife? I thought she was in charge of Weedhaven Middle School?"

"For those of you expecting to see Mrs. Hoehum," the principal continued, "I'm pleased to announce she and her husband have retired and now live in Myrtle Beach. But don't worry. They are apparently in good health and are being helped by the wonderful staff of the Retired Principals Recovery Hospital."

"I've heard about that place," Emery said. "I read about it in the newspaper. Did you know eight out of ten principals suffer from acute anxiety stress disorder? It's true. I looked it up."

"What causes it?" I asked.

"Beats me," Emery replied. "I just read the article. I didn't write it."

"Pssst."

"I hear hissing," Emery said and looked beneath his feet.

"Oh no, it's Jake Pensor. He wants you," Emery said and pointed beneath the bleachers.

"Pssst." Jake hissed. "Get down here, Coldwater. Hurry up. There's going to be a fire drill."

Ding, ding, ding.

A hundred 6th graders, five teachers, and one very worried looking principal dashed for the exits in an explosion of elbows and knees.

One teacher bravely stood her ground.

"Walk," she shouted before finding herself lifted by the crowd of students and carried out of the gym in a throng of dazed and confused 6th graders.

As for me—well, I was too busy rolling on the floor laughing to notice Jake had abandoned me. I was alone beneath the bleachers. And then some conscientious energy saver went and did what people usually do when they leave an empty room—he turned out the lights.

"Help...Somebody...Anybody."

I couldn't see my eyelids in front of my eyes. In fact, it was so dark, I wasn't even sure if my eyes were open or closed.

4

Faced with an utterly hopeless situation, I did what I do best...I screamed.

"Mom."

And when that didn't work, I did what I do second best...nothing.

There I was, hidden beneath the gymnasium bleachers in the dark. Alone—and no way to call for help. I didn't even have one of those buttons on a necklace I could push and shout, "Help. I'm alone in a dark gym and there's no way out. Does anybody know the number to 9-1-1?"

And then I heard rustling.

"Hello," I shouted, and waited. Nothing. And then there it was again. Rustling.

"Who's there?" I shouted. "I know karate."

Which was almost the truth.

I had once asked my mom if I could take karate lessons, and my mom even said yes, provided I stayed out of trouble. But like I've said before, trouble goes out of its way to find me.

According to my mom, who is the resident expert on my little trouble making habit, asking me to stay out of trouble was like asking Charger not to charge the mailman, or asking my little sister Jessie not to act like a little sister.

"I hear you," I shouted into the darkness in response to more rustling. It sounded like somebody was sitting behind me in a quiet theater, digging his hand in and out of a bag of potato chips.

"Hi-ya," I shouted and kicked into the darkness.

Bong!

"Yeow."

Kicking the main support beam of a metal bleacher with your shin never feels good—even when you think you're Bruce Lee.

I fell to the gymnasium floor and grabbed my right shin in a fit of screaming, mean pain that left me squealing from the feeling and wishing I was fishing. And then I gasped for breath as something furry leapt over my face. I stared into the darkness—frozen by fear and pain as the evil monster breathed into my face.

I didn't know whether to panic or sigh in relief. At the moment, it felt good to know the source of the strange rustling sound was a living creature, and not something from the land of the undead. But then again, when it comes to things that go bump in the dark, what difference does it make if your attacker is dead or alive?

And then the lights came back on and the gym was suddenly alive with the sound of bouncing volleyballs and giggling girls.

My eyes stung from the sudden change in the light as I struggled to focus and take in my surroundings.

"What?" I gasped and banged my head against the same support beam that nearly busted my leg, blinked my eyes, and whispered, "Not there." I was staring into the wide, green eyes of a coal black cat the size of a small mountain lion.

"Psst," the cat hissed and karate chopped my cheek with about eighteen razor sharp claws.

"Yikes," I screamed and bolted from under the bleachers. I tried to run, but my legs wouldn't work. Girls were everywhere and I was being pummeled by a million volleyballs at once.

"Get out of here, creep," a girl shouted and hit my sore leg with a ball.

A trail of blood trickled down my left cheek as I dragged my swollen right leg across the gym floor. I must have looked like the *Hunchback of Notre Dame* or something because the girls recoiled in shock, and then erupted in laughter.

"What war did you just come home from?" a wise cracking 8th grader said, followed by another wise cracking 8th grader who claimed, "Don't worry. We're not laughing with you, we're laughing at you."

Welcome to middle school, I thought as I dragged myself to my homeroom.

5

"Jason Coldwater. Jason James Coldwater," Miss Bickerstaff called as I limped into my homeroom.

Emery and Jake sat in the back row of the classroom, grinning like the Cheshire cat in *The Adventures of Alice in Wonderland*."

"Jason Coldwater, I presume?" Miss Bickerstaff said and checked a box on her attendance log. "You're late."

"Better late than never," I said and dragged my wounded leg towards an empty desk next to Emery. "Besides, somebody turned the lights out in the gym. I was trapped. And then a black cat the size of a Buick attacked me."

"Hey, I know that cat," Jake said from the back row. "Did it have green eyes and about 18 claws on its front paw?"

"Enough," Miss Bickerstaff said and slammed a yardstick onto her desk. "Enough of this nonsense," she said and pointed to an empty seat in the front of the classroom. "Sit up here, next to Becky Housman. You look like the type of student that bears considerable watching."

"Who me?" I asked in my patented 'little ole me never causes trouble' befuddled expression.

"Yes, you," Miss Bickerstaff replied. "And while you're at it, perhaps you can explain where you were during the fire drill?"

"Ah, I was in the gym," I said and pointed at Emery and Jake. "I was with them."

Jake shook his head and waved his hands. "Don't look at me. I was minding my own business."

"I think he fell down during the mad rush from the gym," Emery said and rose to address the class like he was Abraham Lincoln giving the *Gettysburg Address.* "We really should practice fire drills more often," he continued. "People need to learn not to panic."

"Are you running for Fire Drill Captain, or something?" Miss Bickerstaff said. "Sit down and shut up."

Great, I thought and fished a cream filled snack cake out of a lunch pack carelessly left lying on the floor next to my desk.

"Hey," that's my lunch," Becky whined and hit my scratched face with the spine of her math book.

"How was I to know that?" I said and jammed the rest of the snake cake into my mouth. I gulped, licked my lips, caught my breath, and returned Becky's glare.

Man that cake tasted good.

"Stay away from me, creep," Becky said and tossed her ponytail over her shoulder. "I hope you get worms, or something."

"More like cat scratch fever," Jake snickered from the back row and beaned me on the back of my head with a spitball. "You could have at least shared your snake cake with your pals."

6

By now you're probably thinking, what more could possibly go wrong for Jason? Or, perhaps you're thinking he has already exceeded his quota of trouble making for one day.

You would be wrong.

Because you see...Trouble never waddles into your life one incident at a time. No. Trouble travels in packs, and it never waddles—it charges into your life with reckless abandon. And what happened in the school cafeteria that first day of school proves my point.

I was side-stepping through the cafeteria line, waiting my turn for my extra crispy, baked macaroni and cheese with tuna salad surprise, when Principal Thaddeus P. Thornton cut into line in front of me.

"Whoa, big guy," I said and elbowed my way in front of the principal. "No cuts allowed." I was only having fun. I was trying to get to know the guy—like. See if he had a sense of humor. I mean, come on...if the principal wants to cut the line, he's going to, and only an idiot would make a big deal about it.

Principal Thornton stared at me for a moment. His jaw hung open, and for half a second I thought he was going to have one of those coronary things where your heart attacks you.

"Young man," the principal said as he reached over my head to grab his tray of mac and cheese with tuna salad surprise. "What's your name?"

"Er...Jake Pensor," I blurted out. I know. It was a bold faced lie. But Jake had it coming.

"Well, Mr. Pensor," the principal said and grabbed a second tray of mac and cheese with tuna salad surprise, "I'll be calling for you later today."

"I'll be waiting," I threw in for good measure.

I almost felt sorry for Jake. For the first time in his life he was going to be truly innocent of a crime he was about to be punished for. Framing somebody is a horrible thing to do, and I wouldn't recommend it, but for the first time since I woke up that morning, I actually felt good, and even whistled one of my favorite *Bad Company* tunes on the way to my table.

"Pensor," the principal shouted from the faculty table. "Stop whistling. What are you? Some kind of miner bird?"

"Yes sir," I shouted back and snapped my hand to my forehead in a mock military salute.

You know, it's strange how this thing called karma works. When you do nice things for people, the world opens its harms and returns the favor. But when you do evil things, or go out of your way to be mean, the world returns the favor to you. In this case, karma exacted instant payment for my lie.

As I saluted, I lost my balance. It felt like I was living inside a slow motion replay. My feet flew into the air and I felt gravity pulling my butt to the floor.

Crash. Splat.

My precious tray of mac and cheese with tuna salad surprise went airborne, then turned and found its way back to ground—right in my face. I brushed the dry mac and cheese from my face to a chorus of laughter from a table full of 8th grade girls.

"Look, it's that creep from the gym," A girl said and promptly choked on a wad of mac and cheese.

"Don't worry, boy," another girl said. "Remember, we're not laughing with you. We're laughing at you."

"Clean up in aisle four," I mumbled and limped out of the cafeteria hungry. "I sure hope Becky has another one of those cream filled snake cake thingies lying around."

Moments later Jake Pensor stepped out of the boys' restroom and grimaced.

"What's your major malfunction?" Jake said as he trotted up beside me and punched my shoulder.

"Oh, other than being hungry, I don't have a problem," I said and rubbed the charley horse in my shoulder. "I think the principal is looking for you."

7

"Jake Pensor to the principal's office," the school intercom crackled.

Twenty heads turned and gawked at Jake.

"Who gets in trouble the first day of school?" Becky Housman said.

"Beats me," I said and stole a glance at her book bag. My stomach was growling like a hungry Bengal tiger, and I was desperate. "Got anything to eat? Maybe another one of those snake cake thingies?" I said and grabbed Becky's book bag."

"Humph," Becky said and jerked her bag out of my hands. "If you're hungry, why don't eat the macaroni noodle stuck in your ear?"

"Mr. Coldwater," Miss Bickerstaff said and slapped her yardstick onto her desk with a loud smack. "Perhaps you would like to join Mr. Pensor."

"Ah, no ma'am," I said and dug the tip of my pinkie finger into my ear. Sure enough, a ripe macaroni noodle was lodged against my ear drum.

"That was not a question," she said and stared at me over the top of her horn-rimmed glasses. "Go. Now."

"Welcome to the party," Jake said as he led the way out of the classroom. "What'd you do?"

"Not a clue," I said. "What'd you do?"

"Came to school," Jake said. "This place is more twisted than a warped pretzel."

Jake was a classic example of a hard luck case. No matter how he tried, things just never worked out for him. Thirty seconds later Jake and I stood in front of Principal Thornton's desk.

"Who are you?" Principal Thornton said and pointed at Jake.

"Ah, Jake Pensor."

"No you're not," Principal Thornton said and pointed at me. "That's Jake Pensor. We met in the cafeteria."

I felt like crawling under the principal's desk, or taking one of those long walks off a short pier.

"If you're Jake Pensor, who's this?" the principal said.

"Er, my name is Jason Coldwater."

"No. You're Jake Pensor."

"No, I'm Jason. That's Jake."

"Then you lied to me?"

"Well, that depends on how you define 'lie,'" I said. "Lie is such a bad word. The way I see it, it was a clear cut example of youthful indiscretion. Harmless in itself, and perhaps even a bit funny when you think about it..."

Principal Thornton allowed me to ramble on for about thirty seconds and then waved his hand. "Quiet. Principal Hoehum warned me about you. You're an incorrigible trouble maker, and I've already taken the liberty of putting your mom's phone number on speed dial. Wheedle your way out of this one, Jason James Coldwater."

Principal Thornton tugged on the ends of his bow tie and took several deep breaths through his nose.

"Is your heart attacking you?" I asked. I was genuinely concerned. He looked like a serious health hazard. "Perhaps you should lie down, or consider joining Principal Hoehum at that rest home for stressed principals down at Myrtle Beach."

"I was thinking more along the lines of a good paddling," Principal Thornton said and sighed. "But sadly, we can't use the paddle anymore. Instead, I'm assigning you to cafeteria duty. You'll help wash the dishes, mop the floors, and carry out the trash."

I groaned, but truthfully, it was all show. I loved cafeteria duty. It was the best way to get seconds.

"That's not fair," I said and stomped my foot.

"It's fair," Principal Thornton said and smiled. He was happy with himself for dreaming up a punishment that "got my attention."

"Now, get out of my office."

Jake wasn't famous for brains, but he wasn't an idiot either. "I'll get you," he whispered. "You tried to frame me."

"Yeah, but if you want seconds on dessert, you need to act nice," I said and skipped back to class. Of course, that was before I found out about the new health and food safety laws.

8

"Oh, this is bad, the head cafeteria lady said and shook her head as she scanned my school record. "You'll have to see the school nurse before you can work in the cafeteria."

"Do you realize how important it is for food handlers to be healthy?" the school nurse said. "You've probably never heard of a lady named Typhoid Mary," the nurse said and checked several boxes on my school health chart. "She had typhoid and spread the disease to dozens of other people because she refused to be treated."

"I don't have typhoid," I said. "What's typhoid?"

"Oh, typhoid is a deadly tropical disease. As is Yellow Fever. You'll have to get vaccinated for both before you can work in the cafeteria."

"I've had my shots," I protested.

"Not these," the nurse said and pulled two ugly looking syringes and needles from a locked drawer. "You just have all the shots for being a student, like measles, mumps, and small pox. Food handlers have to have shots to protect them against tropical diseases."

"But we're nowhere near the tropics," I said and rubbed my arm. This was getting serious.

The school nurse pulled two vials of liquid from a small refrigerator hidden under her desk and plunged the needles into the serum. "Are you ready?"

"I don't think so," I said and slowly rolled up my shirt sleeve.

"Oh, no. Typhoid and Yellow Fever shots have to be injected in a large muscle. You'll need to drop your drawers and bend over."

My face must have turned three shades of purple. "Did you say, drop your drawers?"

"Yes, she did," Principal Thornton said and smiled as he walked past the nurse's office. "And be sure to find something to hold onto. That typhoid shot hurts like the dickens."

Three days later I was cleared to work in the school cafeteria, and it didn't take more than five minutes for the first batch of students to endear themselves in my heart.

"O-M-G," an 8th grade girl shouted and pointed at me. "It's the creep from the gym."

"That guy's everywhere," another girl said and scowled. "6th graders make me sick."

I felt the heat rise in my cheeks and gulped several deep breaths through my nose. Principal Thornton was right. Dealing with students was a pain in the neck.

"Here's your spinach," I said and ladled a heaping scoop of steaming spinach onto one of the 8th grade girl's tray—making sure to spill half of it onto her hand. "Oh, my bad," I said and laughed. "But don't worry. I'm not laughing with you. I'm laughing at you."

"Care for a milk?" I asked and dropped the milk carton into the spinach with a splat. "Don't ever mess with the person who prepares your food."

"Oh, you're a natural," the head cafeteria lady said and patted me on the back. "You have a lot of potential for a rewarding career in the food service industry."

Made in the USA
Coppell, TX
05 October 2020